T0199195

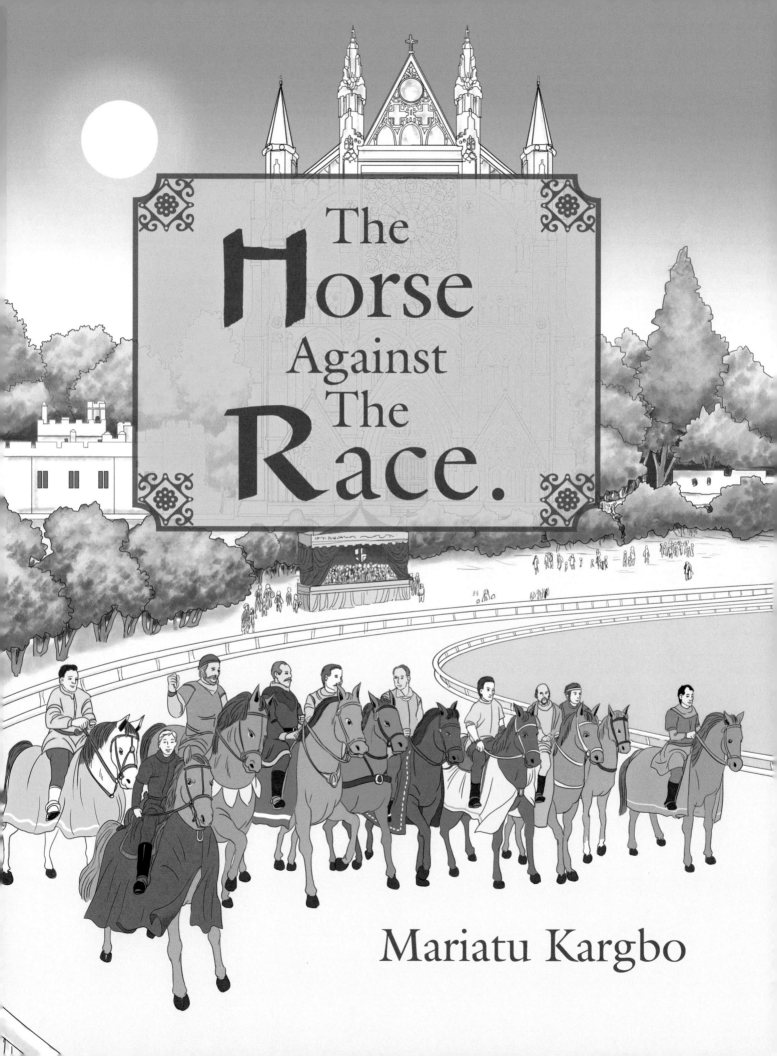

AuthorHouse™
1663 Liberty Drive
Bloomington, IN 47403
www.authorhouse.com
Phone: 1 (800) 839-8640

This book is printed on acid-free paper.

ISBN: 978-1-7283-3051-8 (sc)
ISBN: 978-1-7283-3050-1 (e)

Library of Congress Control Number: 2019915793

Print information available on the last page.

Published by AuthorHouse 10/08/2019

The Horse Against The Race.

By Ms. Mariatu Kargbo, JD, Esq.

Once upon a time in West Minister, Britain, United Kingdom, a medieval village and country, a twenty men horse race occurred on July 4, 1601. The horses, Monticello, Machiano, Machiavelli, along with seventeen other race horses all together raced in Montenegro Ball Park.

The heat in the smouldering near by village of West Minister, by the Abbey, was high as the horses, jockeys, friends, participants, crowds, Monarch kings and queens, reached exceedingly high levels of excitement for the race horses at this year's festivities. The fun loving people full of joy and laughter pleased with pronouncements of festive foods and race horses.

On your marks," will be heard in twenty minutes as the announcer told the enthusiastic crowd.

As the crowd and the twenty Monarchs' horses got ready for the festivities and the horse races, the park full with people, roared with laughter, cheers, and praises for today's festival of the horses against the race. "Fun race," said King Belvoir as the horse crowd cheers in anticipation of the day's events.

Palmero, horse rider and horse jockey, rode the horse Monticello. This horse belongs to Buckingham palace "where warm foods is shared with wealth throughout the kingdom," the outspoken horse Monticello said.

As the three rides men got ready for their race against the horses marathon, Monticello being the first and proper race horse wore proud winter blue decorative clothing and beautiful décor from race horse head to race horse shoes. The red favor cloth covered his head, more red cloth was painted covering his back and stomach. The red draped on his calf foot as the as the red draped all over festive great Monticello Monarch horse from Buckingham Palace horse's best staples. He wowed Hipinishi the Great Queen. He, Monticello, the horse, vowed to win the race against the horses and wowed and wowed his special crowd gatherings. He song his special bread song "all around the horses felt me and all around the horses love me, the people one to one adore me and Monticello," spoke Monticello. The Great Queen Hipinishi's horse song and vowed with grace and honor and "with greatness" tonight and with all, the race is mine".

Polly, the horses rider and horse jockey, rode the horse Machiano. This is from Nottingham Palace, "where God's money bestows me the horse Machiano", the brilliant horse spoke.

Palmetto, the horse rider and horse jockey, rode the horse Machiavelli. This is from the Milky Way Palace "where tonight this gladiator will bring valor," Machiavelli the horse proud and high warned the spectators.

To the surprise of nature and of the Parliament in the country people were allowable of proper etiquette and fine monarch attire clothing, fine wines and fine spectacular of fine race horse people as all got ready for the three horses and the three race horse riders go ready to take to the Montenegro Park for "The Horse Against The Race" fair.

Next, Machiano, the race horse from Buckingham Palace, demurred and well mannered stepped up to the races and gallantly with pure arrogance song his winning song from Abdul and Raven Shatta song writers. "All the horses wins Machiano known and bought sing and praises for the wins and dance song in my house tonight," proclaimed wins horse Machiano. The horse prepared as King Henry rode and inspected the horse with great fan fare.

Last but not least, Pacmoudu, the horse rider and horse jockey, rode the race horse Mankind. Mankind is the horse from Steppenshire, Woodbridge with his pretentious air rode walked and strolled all around the greens getting ready and pickup for the swift ride around the horse races. "He bought money and passed it all around and pleased the crowd," the fun and arrogant horse proclaimed.

For the next chapter of the races, the rest of the seventeen horses all dressed in royal and monarch regalia all gathered for the races with the seventeen horse men and riders as they met with the staple house horses with its favorite.

horse rider Patapsco from Cord Mabatten House Palace cheered warmly the ground as his red regalia spruced up his perfectly well horse fitted regalia body. "Forever the love of the races," pronounced Patapsco.

Pocono, the horse rider and horse jockey, rode the horse Montclair. "The palace of Montclair dominated the newsworthy horse this year as the festive people showed him with love, "vowing" to outshine the competitors as he poured his love and outcry in the race," demanded Montclair.

Peace, the horse rider and horse jockey, rode the horse Mac Child. Mac Child from Fairmont heights village and palace "vowed heavy returns as crowd favorites," mouthed the horse.

Palapalapa, horse rider and horse jockey, rode the horse Montebello. The pretty charismatic horse Montebello called the crowds attention to the undefeated of his home life and fellow horses and horse riders, "esteem is high glazed," Montebello said.

Patay, the horse rider and horse jockey, rode the horse Montclamont. The horse from the palace of Montclamont rode high with other unspoken of winnings, "Make no errors, tonight the horse race is mine," dreamt Montclamont.

Pim, the horse rider and horse jockey, rode the horse Magneto. "Fine, fine all is fine great with me," the horse from the Palace of Magneto spoke.

Polo, the horse rider and horse jockey, rode the horse Monterey. Monterey the horse from the House Palace of Monterey. "Do not be threatened by my fame," the horse Monterrey concocted.

Prince, horse rider and horse jockey, rode the horse Macpeace. "Jockey, jockey, hey, hey, the trophy a lot for the horse, a lot for the win right to the ground," the stallion horse Macpeace from the Palace of Jupiter proclaimed.

Primrose, the horse rider and horse jockey, rode the horse Mac and DoS. "Proud, proud I am but all around horses love me and my mom calls me Sugar," the horse Mac and DoS from Clearing Castle and Palace pronounced.

Paris, The Palm Oil, the horse rider and jockey, rode the horse Mauricio. Mauricio from Gateway Castle and Palace "called the crowds in adoring fever in wishing best and turning crowds heads to Windsor victory as he Mauricio proclaimed wins for one the only and the best," boastfully said Mauricio.

Priest, the horse rider and horse jockey, rode the horse Montpellier. "Sat on my fine greatness horse this fine July day to best awards for this one and only proud horse," accented Montpelier from the Vermont Palace and Castle.

Peter, the horse rider and horse jockey, rode the horse Macintosh. The horse from Liverpool Palace and Castle wrote "long and high, high I have won let it be known and established, tonight the crown's trophy is up to my grabs," the horse spoke riding high.

Palmetto, the horse rider and horse jockey prode the horse McClean. "The decision is on McClean win or lose," the horse McClean from the Carbough Castle and Palace proclaimed.

Pacific, the horse rider and horse jockey, rode the horse Monaco. "Tomatoes, tomatoes, wow, wow, money in my house," as the horse from the crown sultan of Bahrain chimed.

Paseo, the horse rider and horse jockey, rode the horse Mount Sinai from Damsel in Distress Palace. "Wishing on the stars, the only star is Mount from Damsel in Distress Castle," the witting Mount Sinai, the horse beckoned.

Palaver, the horse rider and horse jockey, rode the horse Mount Blanco. "Do not envy my jockey this way or that way," sings the horse Mount Blanco as he waved his calves to victory from the House and Palace of Moumont Castle.

Port Loke, the horse rider and horse jockey, rode the horse Mountain Cut. Mountain Cut from the Palace of Sierra Leone Castle took to praises and warns of outright victory. "Tonight, tonight, greatness watches as Mountain Cut rests easy and knows victory the hearts and minds of my people," roared Mountain Cut.

All royals, all kings and queens all monarch and all palaces and horse racing fans gathered with weary eyes gathered to watch all twenty horses including Monticello overlooking Marley River as the horses the showboating horses ready at the horse's line to win the horse against the races.

The race took two hours as the referee gathered to take all horses though the track with special precautions. Take your mighty feat take it with dare and boldness, tonight is your victory. "On your marks, get ready and go," said the announcer. All twenty horses race through the track, at about equal spreads toward the last twenty seconds, Monticello took the lead and one first place for the Balmont Horse against the race prize followed by Machiano in second place for the Balmont trophy grand prix and third place followed by Mankind.

The end.

Printed in the United States
By Bookmasters